Beginning Again

Beginning Again

A Short Romantic Adventure

Barbara L.B. Storey

SP

Sarman Press

Land Acknowledgment

Storeylines Press enjoys the benefits and blessings of existing on the lands of the Anishinabek, Haudenosauneega Confederacy, and Anishinaabe, Treaty 29, 1827. As settlers to this area, we acknowledge the rights and importance of the Indigenous people and their importance to this region, nation, and its culture, as well as their unjust treatment by the Canadian government and settlers past and present.

Chapter One

HIM

ANDREW STEPPED CONFIDENTLY out his door and headed for the lift. This was the night, had to be. He'd let her go—big mistake in the first place—and then waited too long to get her back.

As much as his friends might mock him for it, he believed she was "the one." No doubt in his mind. He tried not to think about the fact that SHE seemed to have enough doubt for both of them. He just needed to talk to her.

When he got to the street, he headed in the direction of The Angry Dragon, their favourite pub. Hadn't Beckett always said she loved it for the name alone? And they'd both been delighted when they'd found out the food and the atmosphere was as good as the strong, rich single malt Scotch the bartender served them. Funny, that, how they'd both loved Scotch—he'd never met a woman before who savoured it as he did. Was that when he had first experienced the pull of her personality, first known *here was an exceptional woman*? Could be. But every day since then, he'd known it a little deeper, a little stronger.

Why didn't she see it?

As he continued down the street, oblivious to the rush of London's life around him, Andrew thought about that. Why had she turned him down? He'd thought she felt the same way. Maybe he'd taken too much for granted. Because when he'd started talking about commitment, she was the one who'd shied away, gotten "friendly" instead of really listening to him, to what he was compelled to say.

Definitely not what he'd expected. But why—why hadn't he seen her reluctance?

He'd certainly never expected her to just . . . leave. That had left him open-mouthed and stunned. No—this was NOT the way it was supposed to happen. He'd suggested they move in together and had only rosy plans for the future in his mind, and Beckett—well, she'd got that deer in the headlights look and bolted. Leaving him shocked and without a plan B of any kind.

Andrew cursed himself as he thought about how badly he had handled that—mainly because he had been completely unprepared for her response. And so, he had let her go, and now suddenly it was a month since she had quietly slipped out of his life, not responding to phone calls, claiming to be busy when he wanted to talk, and gradually just . . . gone. He was bewildered, and in need of an explanation, if nothing else.

No, he told himself, *I need a lot more than that. I need her.* It came down to that one thing, and nothing else. She was the one, and he had to get her back.

But as he saw the front door of the pub suddenly in front of him, Andrew paused. What if she said no again? What if she turned him down flat, in front of everyone? Because surely all their friends would be there, too. He was the one who had been avoiding the place.

Andrew took a deep breath, grasped the handle of the pub's door, and walked in.

Chapter Two

HER

THE SHEER DIN of the place left her with a headache. Which was odd, because it never used to bother her. The Angry Dragon was one of her most favourite places in the world, had always made her feel relaxed and safe from life's troubles. But the last month . . . .

It was Andrew's fault of course, Beckett thought. He had ruined things by asking her for more. *I'm not ready for more,* she insisted to herself. And yet . . . . This place wasn't the same anymore because he wasn't here. It didn't even seem like the Angry Dragon without him. They'd met here, they'd got to know each other here, celebrated life's joys, big and small, and commiserated on life's ups and downs—all the important stuff. And now, he'd changed all that, damn him. With one stupid question.

And he didn't have a clue what he'd done wrong. Never mind that she was not inclined to tell him—that was beside the point. She didn't want to get serious—what was his problem with that? Weren't most guys delighted to find they were off the hook when it came to commitment? Not Andrew. She smiled in spite of herself. He was an endearing man, and special in so many ways. Why had he spoiled it all?

Beckett groaned when she saw Colin headed her way with a purposeful look and a pint in each hand. Now here was someone who truly couldn't take no for an answer. Why was he so focused on her, when she'd never shown the slightest interest? He seemed to think she was a "project" of some sort, a conquest he could not resist. Andrew had never been that way. . . .

"Here you go!" Colin winked rakishly at her, a move she had seen him perfect many a night in the pub. *Sorry, mate—not buying what you're selling.* She smiled in self-defense.

"Thanks, Colin." She reached into her pocket and brought out a ten-pound note, which she plunked down on the table between them before taking the glass. Making her position perfectly clear. "Just what I wanted—and the next one is on me."

"Oh, no, Becky—I'm buying you a drink!"

Her smile became a bit more fixed. "No, you're not. I've told you how I feel about that before. Colin. Now take the money and drink up. And *don't* call me Becky." She gave him a warning look over the edge of her glass.

"Aww, come on. It's my name for you!" He gave her what he obviously considered his most winning smile. Beckett simply stared at him.

"Not something you get to decide. Now, if you don't want to be told to bugger off, behave yourself and drink your beer."

But Colin's attention was already on someone else, across the pub. *If I'm lucky,* she thought, *he's spotted more suitable prey.*

"Damn me if he hasn't finally shown up. Just when I was making my move."

She didn't want to look, didn't want to know—but how could she *not* know just who he was seeing. And this was NOT what she wanted to deal with tonight.

"Hello, Beckett." His voice was soft, but she could hear it even through the din. He was right behind her, at her shoulder.

Chapter Three

HIM

HE COULDN'T BELIEVE the rush he still got from seeing her, even after a month of confusion and hurt and anger. Damn, he'd missed her, and he wanted badly to think she had missed him, even a little.

Andrew also felt a surge of irritation, bordering on anger, to see Colin camped out there beside her. He was such a transparent wanker, always there to take advantage of a situation. Bastard. Then a thought struck him—this wasn't what Beckett wanted, was it? Someone like Colin, something casual? No. He couldn't believe that of her, even after what she'd said and done. This was just Colin's clumsy way of trying to get laid. *Good luck with that,* he thought, and tried to restrain a smirk.

Colin did not go to the trouble of hiding his irritation, however. "Where the hell have you been?" His voice boomed out over the noise of conversation in the pub, and a few people turned their heads in idle curiosity. "Thought you'd forgotten your way to the Dragon!"

Of course, Colin knew full well what had happened, why Andrew had stayed away. All their friends hung out here, and everyone had known when he and Beckett had parted ways. That kind of news always spreads, whether you help it along with the truth or not. But he was deliberately trying to embarrass Andrew— as was his way—while also pointing out that Beckett was sitting there with him. If he knew her at all, Colin was about to get a nasty surprise.

"Oh, shut up, you twit," Beckett said, and Andrew could not hold back the smile this time. But she did not turn around to look at him—the reaction he had feared and not what he had hoped for. "Andrew is free to come and go as he pleases without you bringing it to everyone's attention. Like I said—drink your beer, stop being an idiot, and behave yourself."

Colin frowned. "Just playing with him," he said grumpily. "And besides, we were having a nice little moment here and he interrupted us. *He* should bugger off, if anyone should."

Beckett put down her beer and glared at him. "You might have been having a moment—with yourself. I was not involved."

Andrew decided it was time to speak up. "I think it's time for you to go be an idiot somewhere else, Colin. I need to talk to Beckett, and we don't need company. So, be a good boy and go bother someone else, okay?"

Colin's jaw dropped.

Beckett finally turned around, giving him a brief nod of appreciation before a look of nonchalance settled back on her face. "What if I don't want to talk to either of you? You can both go have it out somewhere else and leave me in peace."

But Andrew caught something in her expression that gave him hope, and he stood his ground. "No, Beckett, I think we need to talk. I think . . . you owe me that."

She looked him in the eyes, and he could see a wariness there. What had he done to deserve that, to make her so uneasy about his intentions? He had to find out, had to know what had happened between them, even if he couldn't convince her she had been wrong. And she had been.

"I don't want to talk here," she said finally, waving her hand at the crowded pub.

"Then let's go someplace else." He was not going to give in, not for a second.

"You know . . . ." Colin blundered into the conversation, completely ignoring their requests for privacy.

"Colin!" Andrew and Beckett said it at the same time, then laughed together. He could feel her relax just a little. *There's hope.* Andrew turned to Colin again. "Really, Colin, three's a crowd. We'll see you later." Then he very deliberately turned his back to Colin, so that he was finally facing Beckett. "Please."

Chapter Four

HER

SHE HAD HOPED it would be easy to say no to him. After all, she was the one who'd left, so shouldn't it be? But now, as Andrew stood in front of her, asking for . . . what? An explanation? Another chance? All her feelings for him came back, with a force that made her blink.

She missed him. That was the simple truth. She missed *them*. And now that he was here, back in the Dragon, back where they had met, she realised just how much. And if she was honest—that was something she always tried to be—she did owe him an explanation. But did she owe him another chance? That was the real question.

"You really don't want to stay here, find a quiet corner?" She was stalling, and they both knew it.

Andrew snorted. "A quiet corner, in the Dragon? You're joking." Then he paused, looked at her intently, and took a deep breath. "Let's go for a walk, down by the canal."

She made a face; it had always been one of their favourite places to walk, talk, be alone together. Not fair.

"Why are you making me beg?" Andrew asked, his voice soft but with a tinge of hurt she couldn't ignore. "I don't understand," he continued, looking away, "but I want to. I need to."

Beckett sighed and hung her head for a moment. Then took a long drink of her beer. She put it back on the table with a little too much force, and it slopped out and over her hand. "Okay. Let's go."

Colin gave them both a look of disgust, and then finally did as he'd been asked—he buggered off. Beckett watched as he sauntered over to another table and started to chat up Angela.

"Think he'll have any luck there?" she asked Andrew with a tiny smile.

"I don't really care," Andrew said, "as long as he didn't have any with you."

He froze for a moment, and she knew he was afraid he'd said the wrong thing, alienated her. She wanted to reassure him, the instinct coming out of their past, out of the feelings she still had for him, and which, for once, she did not worry about hiding.

"No chance there, to be sure." She smiled at him, and he gave her a hesitant smile back. *This* was not fair—she shouldn't be treating him this way. And all her regrets came back to her in a second— and all her love for him.

"Let's go," she said quietly. "It's too bloody noisy in here." Beckett reached out to touch Andrew's hand, and his smile got stronger. She got up, waved at her friends, and headed for the door.

When they got outside to the street, the pub's noise just an echo behind them, they both paused for a moment. She was unsure how to begin, and wondered if he was, too.

"This way?" Andrew extended a hand in the direction of the canals, eyebrows raised in question.

"Sure," she said, and they headed off, quiet for a few moments.

"You look wonderful," he said eventually.

"Thanks," she said, feeling a surge of awkwardness now they were alone. "You do, too."

Andrew smiled, but didn't say anything more.

The paths by the canal held only a scattered population—an older man walking his dog, a couple here and there, arms entwined, a few teens surely out past their curfew. She was suddenly overtaken by memories of them walking here in the same way, leaning in on each other, talking, laughing, or just being quiet together as they experienced the lapping of the water against the banks of the canal. She missed those times—she could not lie to herself about that.

"So," she said softly.

Chapter Five

HIM

ANDREW DIDN'T ANSWER for a moment, trying to find his way in to what he really wanted to say. Now that he had convinced her to give him some time, let him talk, he didn't want to ruin it by saying the wrong thing.

But was there a wrong thing? he asked himself. They were already apart, she had left him—what worse could happen? She could leave forever, and never give him another chance.

He sighed. They were already close

enough to that he knew there was no real chance of making it worse. *Might as well go for it.*

"So," he said finally, "I asked you to move in, and you ran away. Why?"

Beckett stopped walking and stared at him. "That was blunt."

"Time for a little bluntness, wouldn't you say?" Andrew raised an eyebrow. "I didn't see the point in dancing around the issue anymore." He sighed deeply, shoving his hands in his jacket pockets so he wouldn't reach for her. "I miss you. As lame and dramatic as it sounds, my life is not the same without you. We were so good together—I need to know why you don't feel the same way I do."

Beckett looked at him warily. "Who said I didn't?"

He studied her, disbelief in his eyes and expression. "You're going to have to explain that one to me," he said at last. "You left me the moment I asked for more, even if you were still there, physically."

Becket sighed and started walking

again. He moved to catch up, match her stride. They were silent again for several moments, and then he couldn't hold his thoughts in anymore. "You're confusing the hell out of me. What do you want, really want?"

She kept her head down, her eyes on the path. "Would you believe me if I said I didn't know?"

"Hmm." He pondered that for a moment. "Is that why, then? You turned me down because you weren't sure what you really wanted?"

"I suppose," she said quietly.

"Forgive me, but that seems like a bloody poor way to find out what you DO want, to me!" His voice got louder as he spoke, and Andrew had to make an effort to calm down. He could not blow this chance. "I'm sorry—but I just can't understand this." Another pause. "Do you . . . do you just not love me? If that's the case, I'd appreciate knowing, so that I can stop torturing myself and bothering you." He hated himself for the bitterness that had crept into his tone, but he was scared. Scared of her answer.

Beckett whipped around to face him. She stared into his eyes for several seconds; each one seemed to last an hour to Andrew. He tried not to let the misery that was threatening show.

"I can't blame you for thinking that, really." Finally, she spoke. "And I know I shouldn't have treated you this way, just . . . stopping, without telling you why." Now she sighed heavily, and then slowly reached out to tug on the lapels of his heavy jacket. "I do love you," she whispered. Then, lifting herself up onto her tiptoes, she leaned in and kissed him lightly on the lips.

Andrew was confused, ecstatic, hopeful and wary, all those emotions fighting for control in the moment it took to register that Beckett was actually kissing him again. It was wonderful. It felt like . . . home.

But he couldn't let himself be distracted or think that this was a promise of anything permanent. Not yet.

"That was wonderful," he whispered. It was torture to keep his hands in his pockets, but he knew he had to. "But *why* did you do it?"

Chapter Six

HER

BECKETT COULD SEE the wariness in his
eyes, in his expression. It had taken so
much courage to come looking for her, to
face another possible rejection—and that
was one of the reasons she loved him. He
was not afraid of taking chances. She
wished she could say the same about
herself.

He deserved better, far better than
what she had given him, that's for sure.
She had almost not come away with him
tonight because she was embarrassed by
how she had ended things between them,

just walking away and breaking his heart. He deserved better than her, perhaps. Yet here he was, asking the questions she had wanted to avoid. She owed him answers.

"Because," she said, going back to fussing with his jacket, "it was the only way I could think of just then to . . . begin again." She stole a quick glance up and saw the hope light up in his eyes, just as quickly tamped down as he struggled to keep his expression neutral. "Because it seemed right."

He looked down at her, and she could see he wanted to just accept what she had said and go with it. But he was right—they needed to talk. She needed to try and explain herself, if that was possible. She had treated him badly, and it was up to her to fix it. If that was still possible.

"Come on," she said quietly, linking her arm through his. "You're absolutely right, we need to talk." There was a bench just a few yards away, and she tugged him towards it. "I will try to explain, the best I can."

He moved with her, but did not get

any closer, physically. Wary and definitely holding off on his own feelings until she had explained hers. Once they got to the bench, he sat, half-turned towards her, waiting.

She gave another heavy sigh. "Okay. I do owe you an explanation. Why I . . . left."

"Yes." His tone was not harsh, but she could feel his hurt and a bit of anger.

"And I know I did it in such a cowardly way, and I'm sorry for that, I really am."

Andrew said nothing for a moment, then seemed to relax a bit. "Apology accepted," he said quietly. "And I'm sorry I didn't speak up sooner than this, that I just let it go. It wasn't that you aren't important to me, that WE are not important. I hope you know that. I was just . . . so confused."

Beckett nodded. "I know. But . . . ."

He nodded. "But?"

She fidgeted a bit, staring out at the canal, waiting while another couple walked slowly by. Then she took in a deep breath for courage. "I was afraid." She paused again, searching for the right words.

"Afraid? Of what? ME?" She heard him breathe in deeply, struggling to control himself, to understand. "I'm sorry, but couldn't you have just told me that?" Andrew was keeping himself from moving closer to her – she could almost feel the effort he was making. "Couldn't we have just talked about it?"

"We should have, yes," she admitted. And tried to smile. "But I have a bit of . . . history I never told you about, and it's why I just took off."

He went perfectly still. "History." The word was spoken so quietly,

"And it's completely unfair to you, that reaction, I know it. But . . . I was asked that question once before. By someone who was not as wonderful as you. By someone who hurt me. Not just emotionally, but . . . ." Her voice dropped to a whisper. "Physically, too."

Beckett couldn't look at him just now. She had to get it out before she lost her nerve. "I gave the wrong answer then, and I guess I just don't trust my own choices anymore. I wasn't ready for that question a second time, not even from you. I panicked."

Daring to look up into his eyes at last, she said, "You were too good to be true. So, I bolted, rather than take the chance of being hurt again."

Chapter Seven

HIM

STUNNED. Beyond that, Andrew couldn't even think clearly enough to decide how to react.

How could they have been together for almost a year and he didn't know this about her? There must have been signs, some subtle indication—or not so subtle— that she had reason to be afraid. All he could think of was her confidence, her outgoing nature—these were reasons he'd been attracted to her in the first place.

But now, even as he cast back in his memory for some clue, it hit Andrew that those things he thought of as strengths, as confidence, could also have been carefully constructed defenses. Surely that was what it had been. But he still felt . . . guilty he hadn't figured it out.

He stayed quiet for a moment, collecting his thoughts. He didn't want to say the wrong thing now, at this point where she had been so open and vulnerable. Had finally trusted him. Couldn't risk giving her any reason to abandon him again.

"I. . . ." He paused, bewildered. "Honestly, I don't know what to say. How could I not have known? That's the first thing that comes to mind. Oh, Beckett." He wanted to reach out and hold her but, again, wasn't sure if it was the right thing to do. "I understand why you wanted to keep that to yourself, of course, but I wish . . . I just wish I had known." He stopped again, still taking the news in.

"You didn't, because I didn't want you to know," she said, her voice quiet and sad. "I had to keep that in the past—or at least try to. You were so different, so much more than I had hoped to find, but the fear is always there." She was still holding onto his arm, and she tugged at him then. "It's nothing you've done, if that's what you're thinking. This is about me and my scars."

"Of course," he said automatically. "But I can't help wondering if I triggered something, said or did something that made you feel unsafe?"

"Just ask me to move in with you," she said, trying to make her tone light. "No. Seriously, Andrew—it's not on you. It's my baggage."

He thought for a moment, deciding what to say next. "You could have asked me to help you carry it. Or unpack it. Whatever you needed." He looked over at her. "Not blaming, just saying I would have helped, if I could have."

"But that's it, really," she said, staring out over the canal. "I didn't think you could. I didn't think anyone could. So, leaving seemed like the best thing to do, before it got any worse. Before I said or did something to hurt you."

Andrew looked at her with a raised, skeptical eyebrow.

"You know what I mean." She smiled in spite of herself. "I didn't want to believe you were like him, but . . . it just felt safer to keep it to myself. I was miserable, you know. Every day since I left, I've missed you."

"Have you?" he said quietly. Wanting to believe her.

"Yes." Her answer was firm, no nonsense. "I went about my life, of course, but there were always Andrew-shaped holes in my day." Beckett looked up at him and smiled. "I almost called you a couple of times but couldn't quite do it."

"I wish you had."

She chewed on her lip for a moment. "Me, too. So, when you walked into the Dragon tonight, I was instantly defensive, but also . . . relieved. I knew I had another chance."

Andrew tried to hold it in, but he couldn't. "Forgive me, Beckett, but . . . honestly, you *were* glad to see me? Do you really want to be here with me, now?"

Chapter Eight

HER

BECKETT LOOKED AT HIM, straight into those beautiful honey-amber eyes, and saw his hurt, his confusion as he tried to understand and be what she needed. There was suddenly such a pang in her chest for the pain she had caused him because of her own fears. And she knew she not only had to make it right, she *wanted* to make it right. He was the one—she'd known it in her heart of hearts and just been too afraid to admit it. And had tried to live as if it didn't matter that she'd thrown love away with both hands because of a "what-if"—her oh so precious wall of defense meant to protect her, keep her safe.

Keep safe, from Andrew? With him there was nothing she needed to protect— except his heart.

"Yes." One word—simple, but heavy with meaning and promise. "I would not have left that pub with you if I didn't *know* I'd made a mistake. If I didn't have some glimmer of hope that you might forgive me for hurting you. That you might understand why I hid something so important from you. As soon as I saw you, I knew I had to try, and hope it wasn't too late."

Andrew sighed heavily, relief clear on his face. "Thank god, then," he said quietly. "As long as we're both here because we want to be, I think we're okay." He smiled at her hesitantly.

"I think we're okay, too," she whispered back, then leaned in, still clutching his arm, and snuggled into his coat as a wisp of a chill wind slipped by. "If you can forgive me, that is."

Andrew slipped his arm around her shoulders, pulling her in gently and resting his chin on her head. "It's not so much 'forgive'," he said, his voice still just loud enough to be heard over the sounds of the canal. "Now that I know why, for me it's a matter of understanding. And maybe starting over."

"Mmm." Beckett worked her way under his arm a little more firmly. "Yes, I think starting over is a brilliant idea. Gives me a chance to not be afraid, to make different choices. I don't want to project my past onto my future anymore."

"I like the sound of that word," Andrew murmured. "Here's to our future." He tipped Beckett's chin up, and kissed her—feather-light, no more than a promise, but a promise it was. "I think it could be very bright."

Rather than words, she answered him with her own kiss—a bit bolder, but still not full on, not yet. Beckett couldn't believe how good it was to have her lips touch his again. How could she have ever thought she could live without him? She moved in closer, continuing the contact for a moment longer, and then wrapped her left arm around him, pulling him in.

"That was as sweet and wonderful as I remember," she whispered into his chest.

"Hasn't been that long," he teased. "Did you forget so easily?"

"Not at all," she said with a laugh, and pretended to punch him in the arm. "Seriously?" She calmed down and sighed. "I had to stop myself from torturing myself with the memory of your lips. And . . . other things."

"You're going to make me blush," he replied, chuckling. "But please, do go on—what *else* did you miss?" He poked her with a finger, making her giggle. Ah, yes. Andrew knew all her ticklish spots.

"Oh, there might be a list. Let me think." She teased him right back, and then went for his lips again. But this time he stopped her, pressing his fingertips to her own lips.

"As amazing as it is to kiss you again, maybe we need to talk a bit more first?"

She looked up and saw how much it had cost him to say that. He wanted to kiss her badly. It showed her how serious he really was about this. About her.

Chapter Nine

HIM

HE COULD FEEL HER SHIVER, that's how tightly she was clinging to his arm. Was she really just cold? The wind had picked up, and it was fall. Or was she nervous about talking, about taking a hard look at what had gone wrong?

No. He could not keep second-guessing everything she did or said—they would never be able to start over again if he did that. He had to trust in what she'd said to him: that she wanted to be here with him again, that she regretted leaving, that it hadn't been him she was running from. If he couldn't do that, they really wouldn't have a future.

So, he smiled, stood up, and pulled her to stand in front of him. "Let's go to Mrs. Hillyard's café, get some hot chocolate into us. It's too cold to stay out here."

Beckett smiled, and did a little dance of happiness. "Ooo, I haven't been there in . . . well, you know." Her smile faltered, and she twisted her mouth up in that way he adored. Andrew pulled her in for a quick hug.

"I'll tell you what I just told myself," he said firmly. "We can't start over with doubt or regrets hanging over everything we do. It won't work. Let's just be honest, and do whatever we need to, to get back to us."

She smiled again, and it made him happy to see it. "You're absolutely right. Moving forward!" She stood on tiptoe to kiss his nose, and then linked her arm through his. "Forward to Mrs. Hillyard's awesome cocoa!"

They walked, their pace a bit brisker now, down the canal path and back onto the streets, and in a very few minutes they were at the café. It had always been one of their favourite places to go—other than the Dragon, of course—after a night out, or a film, or when they needed a warm-up, like now. Mrs. Hillyard herself greeted them just inside the door like the long-lost friends that they were. She gave them a few "significant" looks while taking their order, and Andrew had the feeling she was happy to see them together again. He might have been imagining it, but . . . he preferred to go on thinking that all was right with the world again.

Over a few pots of the best cocoa in London, they caught up. Andrew told her about his recent work; as a travel writer, he was obviously away a lot, and he found he couldn't wait to share his adventures in Japan and South Africa with her. He had, in the past, occasionally convinced her to join him for at least part of a trip here or there, as her schedule allowed. Suddenly he had the urge to ask her again. He was leaving for India in a couple of weeks and had the sudden feeling that he didn't want to be separated from her again so soon. *Well, let's see how this goes,* he told himself. No need to rush or ask—*yet.*

Beckett told him about the training she had been doing lately, at her office. It seemed like the up and coming design company was grooming her for big things, but she just blushed and waved away his suggestion that that was the case. He could tell she was pleased he thought so, though.

They had been there an hour and a half when she reached over and took his hand. They had touched a few times since they got there, but this was a deliberate contact, a reaching out that was more than physical.

"So. . . . You really want to take a chance on me again." It wasn't really a question, but there was a bit of something in her voice that told Andrew she was still afraid she had blown it.

"No," he said quietly, and smiled as her eyes went wide. "On us," he said, gripping her hand a bit tighter. "You and me. I've always known we belonged together, and if there are things we need to work out, or weather, I'm up for it. How about you?"

Chapter Ten

HER

SHE SAW the hope in his eyes and felt it in her own heart. Yes. This was what she wanted—a second chance with Andrew. Suddenly she was surer than she had ever been about anything that they belonged together. And what made that feeling even better was that she knew he was sure of it, too.

"I am definitely up for it," she said, her voice quiet but firm. No doubt, not anymore. "And I'm happy, so happy, that you came looking for me, that we can start over. That . . . I haven't lost you because of my fears."

"No, you haven't lost me." Andrew took her other hand in his, held both of them tightly. "I've missed you, every single day. I just wasn't sure if you wanted me to, you know . . . ." He paused and smiled ruefully. "Come after you. Conor said I shouldn't. I should wait and see what you did."

"Well," Beckett said with a roll of her eyes, "Conor is your dearest friend, I know, but he doesn't know a thing about relationships. His history tells us that, doesn't it?"

"True," Andrew said. "But I don't want to talk about Conor now. Or any time soon. I want to talk about you. About us. About what we're going to do next."

Beckett smiled, squeezing his hands while she tried to gather her thoughts. "Where do we begin?" she asked, looking into his eyes again. "I mean, what next? Do we try to go back to the beginning, take it slow? Just go on dates and build it all again, like we'd just met?"

Andrew made an unintelligible noise. "If that's what you need . . . ." She smiled as she saw him struggle to be understanding. She knew he would do whatever they needed to do to get back on track. But it was definitely *not* how he wanted to go, that much was very clear.

"Hmmm," she said, suddenly wanting to tease him, as she always did. "Well, I don't know, there's a certain charm about the idea of being wooed again. But what did you have in mind?" *As if I didn't know,* she thought with a smirk.

His response was so quick, she didn't have time to catch her breath. Andrew leaned across the table and took her lips in a kiss so sweet she didn't want it to end, even if they were in public. By instinct, she raised a hand to cup his cheek while she returned the kiss, measure for measure. Damn, but it was SO good to be kissing Andrew again. *Whatever made me think I could actually give him up?*

She could tell he didn't want to stop—nor did she—but they were in Miss Hillyard's cafe and being in the corner didn't mean they were invisible. With a deep sigh of regret, she pulled back and settled into her chair again. A quick glance told her that the proprietor *had* been watching —with a great deal of approval—as their kiss progressed from an impulse to a reunion that needed more privacy to be fully explored.

"That was lovely," she murmured, once again bringing her hand up to caress his cheek, brush back the dark curls from his forehead.

"*That* is where I want to start," he said, "though preferably without an audience." He nodded in Mrs. Hillyard's direction, and Beckett couldn't contain her amusement. "But that's up to you," he continued. He was still holding her hand and searching her eyes. "Are you ready to pick up where we left off?"

Beckett took him in for a moment: his handsome face, his clear, truthful eyes, his heart so clearly on display in them, and his hope. She got up from her chair, never letting go of him, pulling him up with her. "Yes, I am. My place, or yours?"

"Yours," he decided without hesitation. "You'll be more comfortable there, I reckon?"

She nodded with gratitude. When they walked up to the counter to pay, Mrs. Hillyard waved them off.

"I'm that happy to see you here again, together," she said warmly. "On the house, darlings—just make sure you come back soon, you hear?"

"We will," Beckett promised. She tucked her arm through Andrew's again and they slipped out the door and into the night, headed for her flat.

Chapter Eleven

HIM

IT WAS a bit colder when they left the cafe, and Andrew was all right with that, as Beckett cuddled even closer to him. He could scarcely believe it had all gone so well; in truth, he had come prepared for a fight, a confrontation of some sorts where he had imagined himself arguing his case and convincing—or even begging, a little— her to give him another chance.

An explanation for why she had left so abruptly was something he had hoped for, but never had he imagined what she had told him. He could understand why she hadn't confided in him, or just flat out told him, but it was good that it was out in the open now, and they could go on. Of course, he couldn't help wanting to go find the bastard who had done this to her, and give him some of his own, but that would not be what Beckett wanted, surely. Better to just go on with their lives, and not look back.

"You're awfully quiet." She tugged on his arm as they walked down the street, their steps a bit faster now because of the temperature and, he hoped, the desire to get back to her place as soon as possible.

"Thinking," he allowed, but went no further. He certainly wasn't going to tell her he wanted to go all cave man on some unknown creep.

"Penny for them?" She tugged again, and he smiled.

"Nothing that you can't guess, I'm sure. Glad to be here, with you again. Glad you didn't turn me down. Very glad we're going to your place." He wiggled his eyebrows at her before adding, with a laugh, "My place is a wreck, anyway. Stuff from the last trip not put away yet, trying to pack for the next one."

"You are a bit of a slob, I can't lie," she teased back. "I hope this reunion wasn't motivated by a desire for help with house-cleaning!"

He laughed out loud. "Certainly not! I know better than that." He put his arm around her, keeping her close to his side. "But I wouldn't subject you to it right now, either. When I get back from the next trip, I'll . . . get some help putting it into shape, and we'll have dinner there, okay? To . . . celebrate."

Now she looked serious. "When are you going to India?"

"Not for two weeks, so let's not think about it just now, okay?" He leaned down to kiss her hair, and was distracted for a moment by the beautiful, familiar smell of lemons. He'd always loved that scent.

A few minutes later, they arrived at her flat, and he had to let go of her as they climbed the narrow stairs to the second floor. *You are a bloody goner*, he thought when he found himself smiling at the familiar creak of the second stair from the top, the one they'd always tried to avoid, giggling, when they came back from a late night at the Dragon. Beckett's next door neighbour, a "respectable" matron who took it upon herself to oversee the behaviour of her fellow tenants, always seemed to be listening, and would give him a deep and forbidding frown whenever she saw him leaving Beckett's apartment on a Sunday morning.

"We're here," she said, unnecessarily, as she fitted the key into the lock. "I'm sure Mrs. Islington is marking down the time."

He laughed out loud, and Beckett shushed him. "I was just thinking about her," he stage-whispered. "How did you know?"

"Because it's our tradition, isn't it?" she whispered back. "This is . . . what we do."

"It is," he answered, all humour gone as he looked down at her, loving her, her face, her voice, everything about her and her world, up to and including the nosy Mrs. Islington. "It is most definitely what we do."

They couldn't take their eyes off each other for a moment, and then Beckett turned, a bit flustered, back to her door. It was open in a second, and they were—at last—inside.

Chapter Twelve

HER

As soon as they crossed the threshold, Beckett thought her flat seemed different. No, not different—back to what it used to be like, because Andrew was there. She'd missed him and returning home with him brought back strong feelings and a sure sense of how much a part of her life he was and always would be. And made her question her sanity again for ever running away from him in the first place. He was different from anyone else she'd ever been with.

And now, she thought, *he's back here where he belongs.*

A little voice of doubt niggled at the back of her mind, wondering if this was the right thing to do. *Too soon? Were things moving too fast?* But in the end, she knew that the only way to find that out was to be here, together again.

She turned and smiled at him. "Take your coat?"

He smiled back. "I know where it goes." But before he took it off, he reached to help her get hers off, then turned to open the shoebox of a hall closet where it would hang, and then hung his beside hers. It was such a familiar, everyday gesture, her heart tightened in her chest from happiness.

And then they were standing there, facing each other in her flat. A bit of inevitable awkwardness crept in between them. *What next?* The question was in both their eyes. *Where do we begin again?*

Andrew reached out first. "How about a cup of tea?" he said softly. "We can sit and sip and...."

"More talk?" she asked, reaching out to touch his cheek.

"If you like," he said, a teasing note in his voice. Then his expression grew serious. "Honestly, darling, whatever you want. I know this is a bit awkward, and I don't want to rush anything. Well"—he rolled his eyes and grinned— "I wouldn't mind that, if I'm honest. But the main thing is, I don't want to spoil anything, now that we're here. Now that you've . . . let me back in." He paused and let out a huge sigh. "I feel like I'm learning how to speak all over again. Sorry." He took her hand, brought it to his lips, brushed a kiss across her palm tenderly. "I just don't want to mess anything up."

Beckett looked into his eyes, saw the love and concern and that tiny bit of nervousness and fear in them. She stepped forward and wrapped her arms around him. "I hope we're not that fragile, love," she murmured. "And I'm the one who messed things up, really. I think we should just concentrate on fixing that, and not worry so much."

"Nothing to 'fix'," he insisted, hugging her tighter to him. "Let's just say we took a wrong turn, and we're back on the right track again. And see what happens now."

She looked up at him and knew suddenly what she wanted. Raising up on her toes, she kissed him. Gently, the first time, and then with a little more insistence. He needed no further encouragement, dipping down to make it easier for her to reach him, tightening his embrace, matching her passion with his own. It was several minutes before they stopped, in need of air.

"Sod the tea," she whispered, taking his hand and leading him toward the bedroom.

He followed her, not dragging his feet certainly, but once they were in the dark room, he stopped, hesitating.

"Are you sure, Beckett?"

"We wouldn't be here if I wasn't, Andrew. Please, stop worrying." She turned and took his face in her hands. "We need to get past the 'what a mistake we made' stage and get back to . . . just being us. Like you said. That's what feels right to me. Taking a step back from being 'us' just doesn't make sense. Let's just pick up where we left off." As she spoke, Beckett had started undoing the buttons on Andrew's shirt, slowly, watching for his reaction as she spoke, seeing that he wanted this as much as she did and was only holding back for her sake. "Don't treat me like a china doll," she whispered.

With a groan that made her shiver—god, how she had missed that sound and not even realised it—Andrew took her in a kiss again, his hands busy slipping under her jumper, smoothing across her skin, reacquainting himself with her body. And she wanted to do the same. His shirt finally undone, she pushed it off his shoulders as they kissed, wanting, needing his body against hers again. *NOW*.

Chapter Thirteen

HIM

ANDREW FELT DIZZY. And almost drugged, just holding Beckett in his arms again. When he'd set out for the Dragon that night, he'd not really known what to expect, where he or they would end up. Of course he had hoped for this —exactly this—but a part of him didn't dare believe things would go so well. That he would get her back. But here they were.

He groaned, then bent to pick her up in his arms. Breathless but smiling, he carried her over to the bed and playfully dropped her onto it, as he had always done.

"I want to see you naked," he whispered. "Now."

"Likewise," she said, her voice husky and her breath also coming in short gasps. "What are you waiting for?"

Quickly Andrew got rid of the rest of his clothes, watching as she did the same —only she was slower, and he knew she was teasing him. Again, just as they had always done before. *Stop thinking about before, you idiot. This is now.*

He was finished and naked before she was, which seemed to fit her plan nicely. He grinned as she slowly lowered her knickers down over her hips, making the moment when he would finally see her again stretch out until he couldn't stand it anymore. "Please, Beckett," he murmured.

"You don't have to ask," she said. In one final tug, she got them off and laid back on the bed, arms over her head, posing for him. "I'm all yours." She took him in, eyes roving over his body, remembering him and—he hoped—

finding him just as she had left him. In love with her and ready to be in her bed again. "Come here," she whispered, beckoning to him.

He was on top of her in a second, and their arms and legs were a tangle for a moment before they settled back into their own special fit—even their bodies knew they belonged together. She wrapped her arms around him, holding so tight, it seemed she might be afraid he would go.

"It's all right, darling," he whispered in her ear. "I'm here, with you, and I'm never leaving you again, no matter what."

And then he kissed her—a long, deep, soulful kiss. He was so hungry for her, he could barely think where to start, except for that. After several moments, he pulled back to look down at her.

"I love you," he said quietly. "I want to make you happy for the rest of our lives. Will you let me do that? Do you want that, too?"

Beckett caressed the side of his face, returning his look of love. "Yes," she said simply. "I want that. And I want to do the same for you, if you'll let me."

"It's all I ever wanted," he told her, and bent his head to take her mouth again. But he didn't stay there long. Slowly, deliberately, he moved down her body, paying special attention to the right side of her neck where it joined the shoulder, an especially sensitive area for Beckett. She gasped and arched so that he could reach it properly.

"Christ, that feels amazing," she said, panting and stroking his back to urge him on. "Don't stop!"

But Andrew had other destinations in mind and didn't stay in that spot long before moving down to nip at her collarbone, plant a kiss in the middle of her chest, and then slowly—wanting to torture her just a bit—he moved over to one of her nipples, just grazing it with his lips and then breathing on it.

"OH!" Beckett's back arched up off the bed, and she wriggled under him.

"Shhh," he soothed her. "I'll get there, in my own time."

"You love to torment me," she accused him, but she was giggling by now, clearly showing she loved it just as much as he did.

"Do you want me to stop?" he asked, his voice innocent, and he began to pull back as if he would stop.

"Don't you dare!"

"I thought so." Andrew smiled and bent again to take her now-stiff nipple into his mouth, sucking hard. Beckett's scream was his reward.

"Shhh," he said again. "Quiet. You don't want to get Mrs. Islington all bothered, do you?

"I don't give a damn about Mrs. Islington," she said between gasps. "And I don't care if she's bothered, just don't stop!"

Chapter Fourteen

HER

IT HAD BEEN a month since Andrew had touched her, and right now, that seemed like an eternity ago.

She cradled the back of his head as his lips continued to torment her breast—her skin was on fire, and he was the only one who could both fan the flames and put them out. This was . . . heaven.

There was fear, yes, but it belonged to the past, not to now. Andrew would never hurt her, and she had not trusted her truest instincts when she ran from him. She wouldn't make that mistake again.

Beckett promised that to herself, to both of them.

She moaned, not caring how much the sound might carry. Andrew was moving down her body with his lips; abandoning her breasts for now, but she knew he'd come back to them. She knew his preferences, and he'd always loved that part of foreplay. He trailed kisses, licks, tiny nibbles down the centre of her body, pausing every once in a while just to breathe on her skin—he knew how much she loved that sensation. Beckett shivered, then clenched her fingers in his hair.

"I can't believe how good that feels," she murmured.

"Me, too," he whispered. He came back up to kiss her on the mouth again, looked into her eyes. "I . . . I think the first time might be quicker than I'd like, because all I want right now is to be inside you."

She shivered again, smiled, nodded. "Yes," she said quietly.

"But I promise you"—he resumed his trail of kisses down her body—"that the second time I will be much, much more . . . attentive." He smiled up at her from his vantage point somewhere just around her waist.

"And the third?" she said, teasing him.

"And the third," he replied with a wink. He planted a very sloppy kiss on her navel, making her giggle when he blew a raspberry against her skin.

"Promises, promises," she gasped. "Just . . . go!"

He moved again, so that he was lying on top of her and they were again eye to eye, lips to lips. "As you wish," he said softly. "Always, as you wish."

Rising to his hands and knees over her, he reached over towards the night-stand, opening the drawer and searching with his hand but never taking his eyes off her. She loved the sensations, the thrill of his body on her, over her. *How did I go without him in my life for a whole month?* Now—and thank goodness she had a second chance—she knew that she never wanted to be without him again.

He pulled out a Durex from the

drawer and held it up triumphantly. "You still have them—thank God!"

"What, did you think I was going to get rid of them?" She laughed.

"Maybe you still had some hope," he said, pausing for a moment and looking into her eyes with his own hope shining.

"I think I did," she said, realising as she said the words just how much hope she had kept in her heart. "I love you, Andrew Baine."

He took in a deep breath, and she could see a peace settle onto his face that she had not yet seen tonight. She knew with a certainty that everything was going to be all right now.

"And I love you, Beckett Smythe," he said, his voice clear and firm. "I always will."

He swooped down for a kiss, and then quickly got the packet opened, smoothed it down over his cock. She watched him eagerly, and then wrapped her arms around him as he settled back into place over her. His hand moved down between their bodies, and she gasped and arched up when his fingers slipped into the cleft between her legs and stroked her gently.

"Oh!" She clutched him tighter to her as his fingers moved, bringing her to a state of excitement that felt so familiar, so necessary. All she wanted was what he had promised a moment ago—him inside her.

"Please, love." She breathed the words into his ear and wrapped her arms around his shoulders. "Now!"

And a second later, with a grunt of satisfaction, he buried himself deep inside her, and she knew nothing would ever feel as amazing as making love with Andrew.

Chapter Fifteen

HIM

ANDREW'S GROAN shuddered all the way down his body as she surrounded him, tight and hot. There had been a time when he'd feared he would never feel this again, never know the joy of making love with Beckett again, and he could hardly bear the thought. Now that they were here, together, joined in that way so natural and so spectacular, there were no words to describe it. Any attempt would sound trite, ridiculous—the truth of what they were together needed no words, anyway. It just was, and it was glorious.

"Beckett." He sighed her name as he began to thrust into her—slowly at first, so he could savour every sensation. He lifted up on his hands so his view of her was better but did not slow his pace. Her response was to wrap her legs around his hips, keeping his body tight against hers.

"No worries, love," he murmured, and then bent to kiss her again, exploring her mouth, tasting her and memorizing everything about her all over again. It was bliss, and he began to move a bit faster inside her, a bit deeper with each stroke.

"Oh!" Beckett's cry was muffled against his lips, and he stopped their kiss to search her face, suddenly anxious.

"You're all right?" he said quietly. It had come back to him, just then, her reason for leaving him, and he wondered if they were moving too fast. Not that they both didn't want to be exactly where they were—that was pretty plain—but if this stirred up memories . . . .

"I'm fine, darling," she whispered, tracing his lips with her fingertips, her breath coming quickly. "Don't worry about ghosts, forget how stupid I was. Just make love to me, please."

"With the greatest pleasure," he said, smiling. "It's all I want to do." And he came down on his elbows so that their skin was touching—sweaty and sticking together and glorious. Andrew began thrusting again, faster and with more force, till every stroke jarred them. They were both panting now, hands everywhere, as if wanting to reassure themselves this was really happening, really true. They were back together. And nothing would ever part them again— Andrew could not even think of it happening.

Beckett wrapped her arms around his shoulders, clinging to him so she could better meet each thrust with a push of her own, driving him deeper inside her.

"Damn! You feel so good, Beckett, so incredibly good." He kissed her again, briefly, and then began to lay trails of soft, quick kisses all over her eyelids, cheeks, nose, everywhere. He nuzzled at her neck again, making her squeal when he nipped her gently in her sensitive spot. "You're so good I could eat you," he breathed into her neck.

"Well, I am hoping for that chance a bit later." She laughed and then gasped when he tweaked her nipple.

"I love it when you're naughty." Andrew smiled and kissed her nose again. "God, I've missed you."

Beckett went quiet for a moment, and her face was serious. "Don't let's talk about that, okay?" she said, her voice so low he could just hear it. He stopped moving and took her face between his hands.

"Don't you ever think I'm reminding you, or judging," he said, panting slightly as he forced himself to hold still for a moment. "You had a reason to be afraid. And it doesn't matter now, anyway. We're here, and I just wanted you to know how happy that makes me. Ecstatic is more like it. I love you and it's the best thing that ever happened to me, that you were willing to tell me your fears and give us a second chance."

"It was never you. You know that,

right?" She seemed worried, wanting to be sure he understood.

"I know that now," he reassured her. "And you're right, we shouldn't look back, only forward, darling." He swooped down to kiss her soundly. "And you have no reason to feel guilty."

She smiled and kissed him back. "I know what I'd rather feel," she said, and tightened her legs around him. He could feel her moving her heels to hook around each other, and then the pressure as she dug them into his lower back. "Go on," she whispered. "We were just getting to the best bit."

He laughed. "Again—as you wish, my love."

Chapter Sixteen

HER

BECKETT LAUGHED, a strong sense of relief coming over her as they fell back into the habits and endearments and sense of comfort with each other they had always had, and which she'd thought lost to her. Thank goodness her fear had not driven Andrew away forever.

She gasped as he moved faster, a bit rougher as his control started to give way. *This* was the passion she remembered, the intensity that was like nothing else she'd ever shared, with anyone. She clasped Andrew more tightly to her, wrapping her arms around his shoulders to stay with him in this familiar rhythm, feeling their sweaty skin stick together and come apart as they moved. Thank goodness he had come to the Dragon tonight and changed her life—again.

"Oh, my love," she murmured, unable to come up with anything more coherent. Andrew responded by burying his face in that soft meeting place between her neck and shoulder that he had always favoured. A moment later she felt his lips gently nibbling at her collarbone.

"Never giving you up again," he whispered against her skin. His thrusts slowed a bit, went deeper, harder, and she knew he was near his release. Slipping his hands under her, he lifted her up so that he could kiss her more easily.

"Try and get rid of me," she whispered back between kisses.

He laughed, and then she laughed, too, both of them caught up for the moment in the sheer joy of being together again, heart and body and soul. Andrew kissed her again, and then moaned and began to speed up.

"Sorry, love," he panted, "I think I'm not going to last too much longer. You're too delicious, I can't—"

"No worries, darling," she sighed. "It's just what I want, too. Don't hold back." She wanted, more than she could tell him with words, to feel Andrew lose himself in her, as he used to. To come apart at her touch, as she did under his. Urging him with hands and lips and wrapping her legs more tightly around him, Beckett whispered and cried out and demanded more —and gave him all of herself as well.

A moment later, he gasped and went rigid, and then the pulse of his release filled her, a sweet sensation she thought she'd left behind forever. She almost wept, her love for him was so intense at that second. And then she couldn't breathe as her own orgasm rolled through her, taking her by surprise with its strength. Her stomach had knots and butterflies at the same time, her toes curled, and she was gripping Andrew so tightly with both arms and legs she was sure there would be bruises on his fair skin.

"It's all right, love," he murmured, covering her face with quick, soothing kisses. "I have you." He rolled over onto his side, bringing her with him, and they lay there for a moment, touching, kissing, soaking each other in as their bodies calmed and their hearts stopped racing.

Chapter Seventeen

THEM

FOR SEVERAL MOMENTS the only sound was their breathing. As even that began to settle and quiet returned, Beckett noticed Andrew staring at the wall opposite the bed. Puzzled, she waited for a moment, and then whispered, "Are you all right?"

"Perfectly." Andrew's voice was almost smug with contentment, and he pulled her closer, so that she was half-resting on his chest. "I'm just waiting."

"For what?"

"Mrs. Islington. Any moment now, we

should hear her throwing her shoe at the wall, right about there." Andrew pointed at a spot midway between ceiling and floor.

Beckett giggled, and then hushed herself. "Do you really think she'd still—"

A loud *thump* echoed off the wall, just a foot to the left of where Andrew had pointed. Followed by a second impact, which was a bit louder. They looked at each other, and then burst out in a howl of laughter that almost drowned out a third thump.

"Now I know that all is truly right with the world," Andrew said finally. It had taken a few minutes to get themselves under control, and now he was content to sink into the mattress with Beckett under his arm. "How about you?"

"I'm feeling pretty happy," she said, smiling up at him.

"Happy enough for some more serious talk?" He asked the question quietly, just a touch anxious. "I don't want to spoil the mood, but I think we need to get some things settled." Andrew sighed. "I'm going off on assignment next week, and I have two propositions to make. Want to hear them?"

"Yes, please." Beckett touched his cheek. "I do."

He sighed again, this time in relief. "Okay, good. First, I'd like to suggest that you come with me when I travel." He raised a hand before she could say anything. "Let me finish. You *are* a free-lancer, you can work anywhere, yes? I'm not asking you to give up anything. I'm asking you if you want more. Because I know I do. I don't really want to be without you, now that we've . . . fixed things." He bit his lip for a moment. "Or at least started to fix things. What do you say? Would you at least consider it?"

Beckett let out the breath she'd been holding. "Wow. That's a . . . serious propo-sition. And a big change." She tilted her head, studying him. "Not saying I can't, but I do need to think about it, okay?" Her heart had jumped a little at his words—

both excitement and fear—but the excitement was a wee bit stronger, even right off the bat, so she took that as a good sign. "It's not an ultimatum, is it?" she asked, and found herself holding her breath again. She didn't think Andrew would do that to her, but she needed to feel . . .secure.

"Not at all," he said, reassuring her with a quick kiss. "I would never force you or insist you do anything. This has to be a mutual decision; I'm simply hoping you'll agree with me that it's what we need."

Beckett settled down to nuzzle into his neck again. "Let me think on it a bit, and then we'll talk again, all right? It IS an important decision."

"Fair enough." Andrew's arm tightened around her just a tiny bit, a hug that brought her in under his shoulder.

"What's the second proposition, then?" she asked, ghosting her lips across his smooth chest.

"Hmmm." Beckett could feel the rumble in his chest as he drew the sound out. "Not sure whether I should bring it up right now – maybe I should wait."

"No fair – you can't tease me that way!" She wiggled her hand down between them and pinched his bottom.

"Hey! Abusing me isn't going to get you anywhere," he warned her, attempting to sound stern and offended.

"It always worked before," she said slyly, and started to drag her fingers across his hip, headed in another direction entirely.

"No," he insisted, capturing her hand and bringing her fingers to his lips. "You're not going to distract me with that. If you want to hear it, we're going to do this properly."

"Do what properly?" she insisted. "Tell me, or I'll throw a shoe at you, too!" Her threat could hardly be taken seriously, as she dissolved into laughter as soon as she said the words.

Andrew took her face in his hands and kissed her soundly; this had the effect of completely stopping her laughter, and she sank into the bliss of his warm, soft lips, forgetting her desire to know his secret.

"I love you, Beckett," he murmured. "I don't know that I've ever felt like this before, except maybe when we began. No." He shook his head, and whispered, "This is even better. Wait here – I've got to get something."

Bewildered, Beckett watched him go over and start fumbling through his clothes. "What . . . what are you doing?" She started to laugh, and then saw he was putting his trousers on. "Aren't you staying the night?" she said, her smile fading.

"Of course I am, silly." Andrew turned back to face her. He was holding something in his left hand. "I just thought I should be decent for this bit."

"Decent? Andrew, what are you on about? All I've got is the sheet and I don't intend to change that – why do you need to be dressed?"

"Because it's an important moment. And you look perfect just as you are."

He walked back to the bed, dropped

to his knees, and took her hand in both of
his. The box he held was dark blue,
smooth, and one of its corners dug into her
hand sharply. She winced at the sharp
poke, and then froze. Small, dark, elegant-
looking box . . . .

Andrew took a deep breath. "I'm
taking a chance here, but I've been
waiting to give this to you since . . . well, a
month ago. And I'm as nervous as hell, but
I still think it's the right thing to do. You
don't have to decide on this right away
either, I promise, but I can't wait any
longer to give it to you." He let go of her
and held out the box on the palm of his
hand.

Beckett couldn't breathe, and for a
moment she couldn't sort out what she
was actually feeling. Excitement, joy, and
a thrill of hope collided with nervousness,
fear, and a desire to run. Then she looked
at Andrew and saw the same tumultuous
struggle in his own eyes, and she knew she
had nothing to fear.

Still, it was impossible to keep her
hand from shaking as she reached out and

took the box and opened it. And then gasped. A huge, gorgeous, and impossibly sparkly square diamond nested in a delicate antique setting. There were three small sapphires on either side, all in a row and shining with their own special light. Her favourite gemstone. It was surely something he'd had created especially for her – she'd never seen anything like it. "Oh, Andrew," she whispered, staring at it.

"I have to say the words." His voice was low, rough, and slightly shaky. "You *don't* have to answer now, but I have to ask. Beckett." He paused, taking another deep breath. "Will you please marry me?"

Beckett looked up into his eyes, her lips round with surprise, still at a loss for words.

"Just keep it, for now," he said, sounding even more unsure. "It was never meant for anyone else but you anyway."

She realized, with a great swell of love, how much it had cost him to do this, how nervous he was about her answer. He was afraid he'd made another mistake, but he had done it anyway. He loved her that much.

"Oh, Andrew." She threw her arms around his neck – holding onto the box tightly as she did – and began to breathe again as his arms slipped around her, too. She pulled back just enough to kiss him, and then said, "I love you." Another kiss, this one longer, and then she pulled back to say, "Yes."

He stared at her – now his mouth was hanging open. "You're sure? You really want to— What am I, an idiot? I'm not giving you a chance to change your mind!" He hugged her tight again as they both began to laugh and cry together.

"I won't make that mistake again, darling," she murmured, slipping her hand up into his dark curls and nuzzling against his cheek. "You're stuck with me now."

"Let's make it official, then." Andrew let go of her, reluctantly, and took the open box from her hands. Still on his knees at the side of the bed, he offered it to her with a huge smile and a slight bow of his head. "Will you do me the honour?"

"In a heartbeat," Beckett replied, holding out her left hand. She thought her heart might explode as he slipped the beautiful ring onto her finger. She'd thought their physical love had been fated, but this – this was more perfect and essential than anything she ever had or ever would experience. She knew no more fear or hesitation. Only gratitude that they'd had their second chance at love.

"This is the best moment of my life," Andrew said quietly, staring at her as if he could never take her in, never get enough of simply looking at her. Beckett felt a swell of pure joy well up in her, so strong she couldn't think of words big enough to express it. She jumped forward, sheet falling down around her hips, and wrapped Andrew in the biggest hug ever as she let out a squeal of complete bliss.

Two seconds later, another thump sounded against the wall – and they both collapsed on the bed in hysterical laughter.

It wasn't long before they were both deeply committed to making even more of a disturbance for Mrs. Islington, but if there were any more shoes thrown, they were completely oblivious to them. Beckett and Andrew were lost in their own private world, and they had no interest in leaving it, ever again.

Thank You For Reading!

Dear Reader,

I hope you enjoyed this book - thanks so much for choosing it! The author and I appreciate your support of indie authors and publishers more than you can know.

If you'd like to tell the author what you loved about the book, or even what you didn't, you can write to them care of support@ storeylinespress.com and I will forward it to them. And you can subscribe to our newsletter at www.storeylinespress.com   to keep informed when any new releases come out.

Should you feel so inclined, we'd like to ask you a favour. Would you consider leaving a review of the book? Feedback is so important to authors, and reviews help bring more atten-tion to the book on sites like Amazon, Goodreads, Story-Graph, and others. Reviews are hard to come by these days – but they can make or break a book.

If you do a review, send me the link and I'll give you a free ebook of your choice from our catalog.

Thank you SO much for

reading Storeylines Press books
and for supporting our work.

With our thanks,

Barbara Storey
Owner and Editor in Chief
Storeylines Press

About the Author

Barbara L. B. Storey is an indie author and publisher, a photographer and digital artist. She loves to write, to read, to travel, and she believes in love very deeply. She was born and now lives in Canada but is a former resident of New York City and misses it very much.

She's also particularly fond of certain book series - The Lord of the Rings and Outlander - of poetry, historical fiction, mysteries and thrillers, biographies, and history of almost any kind, but particularly art and political.

She has lived several different lives, but through them all, one thing has remained true: creating is essential. Whether it's with words or images, as long as she is creating, she is happy.

- facebook.com/barbaralbstoreyindieauthor
- instagram.com/blbstoreyindieauthor
- tiktok.com/@storeylines_press
- goodreads.com/barbaralbstorey
- bsky.app/profile/blbstorey.bsky.social

Also by
Barbara L.B. Storey

Finding Our Way

Need: An Erotic Anthology

9 781998 389674